Word List

Here is a list of words that might make it easier
to read this book. You'll find them in boldface
the first time they appear in the story.

strummed	strumd
cymbals	SIM-buhls
bass	BAYS
rhinestones	REYEN-stohnz
lyrics	LEAR-iks
enthusiasm	in-THOO-zee-a-zuhm
idol	EYE-duhl
construction	kuhn-STRUCK-shun
leprechaun	LEP-ruh-kon
impersonating	im-PER-suhn-ayt-ing
amplifier	AM-pluh-feye-er
encouragement	in-KER-ij-ment
opinion	uh-PIN-yuhn
appliqués	a-pluh-KAYS
instruments	IN-struh-ments

Barbie™

Skipping a Beat

Barbie® and associated trademarks are owned by and used under
license from Mattel, Inc. © 1999 Mattel, Inc. All Rights Reserved.
Published by Grolier Books, a division of Grolier Enterprises, Inc.
Story by Lynn Offerman. Photo crew: Joe Atlas, Susan Kurtz,
Tim Gelson, Robert Holley, and Judy Tsuno.
Produced by Bumpy Slide Books.
Printed in the United States of America.
ISBN: 0-7172-8858-7

GROLIER
BOOKS

Chapter One

"Come on, Drew. Let's go," said Skipper, tapping her drumsticks together.

"In a minute," Drew answered. He plucked two strings on his electric guitar and winced. Then he tightened one of the strings and **strummed** a chord. "Okay!" he declared. "Let's rock and roll!"

Skipper counted out four beats on her **cymbals.** Then the small basement studio exploded with the sound of the electric guitar.

The rest of the group joined in. Skipper picked up the beat on her drums. Ron came in on **bass** guitar. Cara played keyboard and sang. She

1

had written the song herself.

The band's six months of hard work were finally paying off. Velvet Groove sounded like a real rock and roll band. It had been hard to find time to practice. Everyone in the band was so busy. Cara was class president and a cheerleader. Ron played football and coached the PeeWee League on the weekends. And then there was Drew, the editor of the school yearbook. He was the cutest boy in school. At least, that's what Skipper thought.

Halfway through the song, Skipper's best friend, Courtney, walked into the studio. Skipper smiled at her. Courtney had a large drawing pad tucked under her arm. Skipper knew she had just come from her fashion design class.

Courtney plopped down on a comfortable chair to listen. Then she took out some colored pencils and began to sketch.

Soon the band finished its practice.

"Great job, guys," Courtney said, jumping up. "You sound better every week."

"Thanks," said Drew. He brushed his brown hair from his forehead. "We still have a lot of work to do."

"The school dance is only a month away," Skipper added. "It's really nice of your dad to let us use his studio for the next few weeks."

"No problem, Skipper," replied Courtney. "You know my dad would do anything to help." She smiled and placed an arm around Skipper's shoulders. Skipper was like a second daughter to Courtney's parents. After all, the girls had been best friends since first grade. They'd spent every summer together at camp. And they slept over at each other's houses almost every weekend.

Drew peeked over Courtney's shoulder. "What's that?" he asked, pointing to her sketch pad.

Courtney proudly held up her drawing.

Ever since she was small, Courtney had loved to draw. "Skipper told me you were trying to decide what to wear  for your first performance. What do you think?" She pointed to the first sketch. It was a drawing of a young man with brown hair. He was dressed in green velvet pants and a green satin shirt with green **rhinestones.** "This is you, Drew," Courtney told him.

"Uh, great," Drew replied flatly.

Skipper could tell that he wasn't too happy. "I guess that's supposed to be me," she said, pointing to the sketch of a blond girl in blue velvet pants. She wore a satin shirt with blue rhinestones.

"Yep. That's right," Courtney answered.

Cara and Ron looked at the sketches.

Neither of them said a word.

"Well, what do you think, guys?" Courtney asked eagerly.

Ron looked at the sketch of himself. He ran his fingers through his shiny black hair and shook his head. "Look, if you think I'm going to wear those clothes . . . ," he began.

"You're absolutely right," Drew quickly finished for him. Ron's eyes widened in surprise. Drew smiled sweetly at Courtney.

"Really?" Courtney asked. "I wasn't sure if you liked them."

"They're great!" Drew replied.

Courtney looked pleased. "I know a thrift shop where I can get almost everything we need for under ten dollars," she said. "And I already have the rhinestones." Courtney glanced at her watch. "Hey, maybe I can get to the thrift shop before it closes. Want to come along, Skip?"

"Sounds like fun," Skipper quickly replied.

5

Secretly, she hoped the outfits would look better after her friend actually made them.

"See you tomorrow," Skipper called over her shoulder. Cara waved good-bye without saying anything. She was listening to Drew and Ron, who were talking softly. Skipper wondered what they were saying.

Chapter Two

The next afternoon, Skipper played a tape of the latest Velvet Groove songs for Barbie. Barbie listened and told Skipper which songs she liked best. Barbie thought some of the **lyrics** were really good.

Suddenly the doorbell rang. Skipper stopped the tape and ran downstairs. She opened the door and saw Courtney standing there with a huge grin on her face.

"Have I got a surprise for you!" Courtney blurted out. "Grab your bag and come on!"

"Where are we going?" Skipper asked.

Courtney's **enthusiasm** was one of the things Skipper liked most about her friend.

"I just found out that Quick Sand is performing live at the mall this afternoon!" Courtney exclaimed.

"You're kidding!" Skipper said excitedly. Quick Sand was one of her favorite bands. Lily

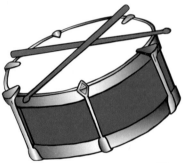

Sands, Quick Sand's drummer, was her **idol.**

"My mom offered to drop us off on her way to the store. Hurry up!" Courtney said with excitement.

Skipper shouted upstairs to Barbie, "I'm going to the mall with Courtney. We'll finish going over the songs when I get home."

The girls hopped into the back of Courtney's mother's minivan.

When they arrived at the mall, a crowd of teenagers was already gathered out front.

"Yikes!" Skipper cried. "It looks like everyone in town is here!"

Slowly the crowd moved through the entrance toward the concert area. A stage had been set up in the center of the main level. Skipper and Courtney were thrilled to find the last two seats near the front.

"Isn't this great?" asked Courtney. "We'll be able to see everything from here!"

Skipper studied the stage. All of the equipment looked shiny and new. Lily Sands's drum set sparkled under the lights.

Suddenly Courtney grabbed Skipper's arm. "Look, there's Drew and the gang!" she said.

Skipper turned around.

"Hey, Drew! Cara! Ron!" Courtney shouted, waving her arms madly.

They looked over and waved back. Skipper's heart skipped a beat when she saw Drew. He motioned to Skipper to come over.

9

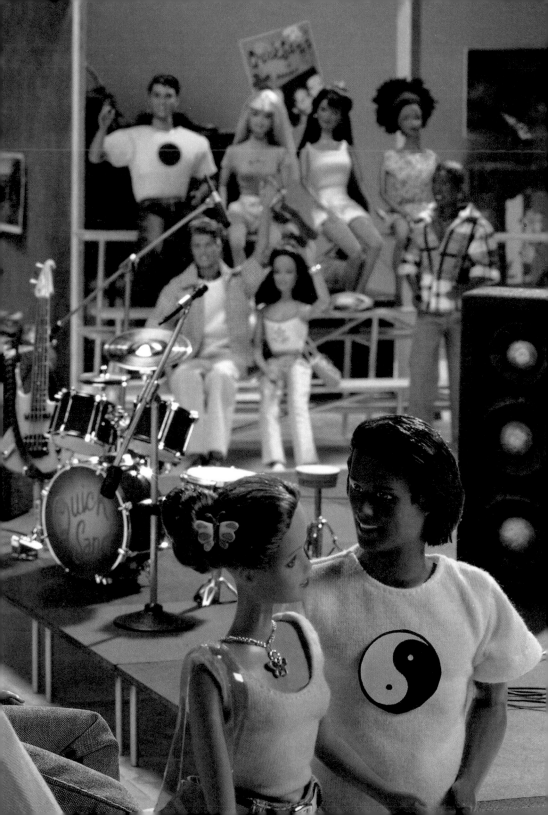

"Courtney, I think Drew wants to tell me something," Skipper said.

"But the concert's about to start!" Courtney exclaimed.

"I'll be right back," Skipper replied. She stood up and ran her fingers through her hair. She quickly made her way over to where Drew and the others were sitting.

"Hi!" Skipper said, slipping into the seat next to Drew. "Isn't this great?"

"We're glad you're here," Cara said. "I called your house when I found out about the concert. Barbie told us you were already on your way."

"Skipper, we've been talking things over," Drew began. "It's about Courtney."

Then a booming voice came over the loudspeaker. "Get ready to rock with . . . Quick Sand!"

The audience applauded wildly as the band

ran onto the stage.

Skipper touched Drew's arm. "Let's talk later," she shouted over the noise. Then she hurried back to Courtney.

Quick Sand's lead singer waved at the audience as he picked up his electric guitar. But it was Lily Sands who held Skipper's attention. She was dressed in black jeans and a black tank top. Her top was covered with small white beads that sparkled under the lights. She wore her shiny black hair in a long French braid.

"Now, *she* looks really cool," Skipper thought.

Listening to the music, Skipper tried to imagine what it would be like playing in front of so many people. Closing her eyes, she could almost feel the heat from the lights on her face. The beat of the music pounded through her brain.

Quick Sand played for about an hour.

When they finished, the audience rose to its feet and cheered.

Skipper had loved every minute of the concert. She thought about Velvet Groove's upcoming performance. She was really excited to be in such a talented band with people she liked. She sneaked a look at Drew and sighed.

"I promised I'd go meet Drew for a minute after the concert," Skipper told Courtney. "He's waiting for me. I'll be right back."

Courtney nodded. "I'll wait here."

Skipper hurried over to her friends in the band.

"We thought we might look in a few stores. Maybe they have some good clothes for the band," Drew told her. "Do you want to come with us?"

Skipper was confused. "I don't get it, Drew," she said. "Courtney's already working on our clothes."

Drew sighed. "I know, Skip. It's just that we really don't like her sketches."

"It's our first big gig," Cara explained. "We can't look bad."

Skipper took a deep breath. "Maybe the costumes will turn out better than her sketches. Come on, let's give Courtney a fair chance," Skipper pleaded. "Otherwise, we really need to tell her how we feel. There's still time for her to come up with some new ideas."

Drew shook his head. "I don't want you to say anything to Courtney, okay?"

Skipper frowned.

Cara broke in, "Maybe we could look for some backup clothes, just in case."

"I guess so," Skipper agreed. "See you later, guys," she said as she waved good-bye.

"What did Drew want?" Courtney asked when Skipper returned.

"Oh, nothing much," Skipper replied.

"How about getting something to eat?" she asked, quickly changing the subject.

"Great," Courtney said. "But I can't stay too long. I've got to work on the band's outfits. I need to get started on them soon."

Skipper forced a smile. "What am I going to do?" she thought. "If these outfits don't look great, the band is going to be really mad. And if we don't wear them, Courtney's going to be really hurt." She grabbed Courtney's arm and pulled her toward the food court.

That night, Skipper saw Barbie sitting at the table looking over some blueprints. Barbie worked as the head architect for a **construction** company. They were designing some new office space. Once the drawings were finished, the work on the new building would begin.

Skipper wanted to talk to her sister about what was going on. But Barbie looked really busy. And Skipper didn't know where to begin.

She thought, "I've got to find a way to handle this myself."

Skipper decided she would talk to Drew at the next rehearsal.

Chapter Three

The next week, Skipper met Drew at the studio. Skipper smiled nervously and thought, "He always gives me butterflies. He's so cute." Then she sighed. "Okay, here I go. I've got to do this for Courtney." She took a deep breath.

"I'm glad Ron and Cara aren't here yet," Skipper began. "I've been wanting to talk to you."

"What's up?" Drew asked.

"Why don't you want to tell Courtney the truth about her designs?" Skipper asked Drew seriously. "She could start working on something else right away."

Drew looked down and strummed his guitar. "If she gets mad, we could lose all this," he replied, waving an arm around the studio. "We'd have no place to rehearse. Maybe we can hold off telling Courtney until right before the dance."

Suddenly Ron came limping in on crutches.

"What happened to you?" Drew exclaimed.

Ron blushed. "I got tackled pretty hard in yesterday's football game. I pulled something in my knee. The doctor says I should be fine in a few days."

"Well, at least your hands are okay," said Skipper.

Ron raised his right hand. He wore a splint on his index finger.

"Oh, no!" Skipper cried. "How are you going to play bass?"

Ron leaned his crutches against the wall and picked up his guitar. "It's just a sprain," he explained. "The splint comes off on Tuesday."

He plucked at his bass with his thumb.

Then Cara walked in. She looked upset.

"Are you okay?" Drew asked her.

Cara sighed and put her hand up to her throat. "Cheering at the football game yesterday strained my voice," she croaked. "I can't sing today. I just need to gargle with warm water and rest my voice for a few days."

Drew buried his face in his hands. "Oh, great! What else could possibly go wrong?"

Just then, Courtney walked into the studio. She was carrying four sparkling outfits.

"Ta da!" she sang, beaming. "I can't wait to hear what you think of them."

The room went silent.

Courtney had done a great job picking out used clothing and decorating it. But even Skipper had to admit that the outfits were way too showy. Skipper looked at the faces of the other band members. She could see the disappointment in their eyes.

Finally Drew spoke up. "They're really something else," he declared.

"Very colorful," Ron added, trying to sound enthusiastic.

"We'll certainly sparkle under the lights!" Cara said in a scratchy voice.

"What do you think, Skipper?" Courtney asked eagerly.

Skipper knew she had to think of something to say. But what? She wondered if Drew was right. "If Courtney gets mad enough," she thought, "she might kick us out of the studio. Then Drew would be really mad at me."

At last, Skipper said, "You did a great job with the rhinestones."

"I'm so glad you all like them," Courtney

exclaimed happily. She handed a costume to Skipper and laid the others on the couch. "I'll leave them here so you can try them on." She glanced at her watch. "Oops! I'm late for my class! See ya!" Courtney bounded up the basement steps.

When she was gone, Ron turned to Drew. "*Now* what do we do?" he asked.

"I'm not sure," Drew sighed. He held up the green outfit and slowly shook his head. "We are *not* wearing these!" he said. Then he glanced at Ron's bandaged finger and Cara's unhappy face. "This isn't turning out to be much of a rehearsal," he chuckled. "Let's call it quits for today. We can talk things over tomorrow."

Skipper waited for Barbie on the front steps of Courtney's house. She was happy to see her big sister's blue van pull up. Barbie always knew how to make Skipper feel better when she was upset.

"How did rehearsal go?" Barbie asked as

Skipper hopped into the passenger seat.

Skipper rolled her eyes. "Awful," she groaned. She told Barbie about everyone's troubles and about Courtney's costumes.

"I see," Barbie said. "So why don't you break the news gently to Courtney? Sometimes it's not what you say but the way you say it that matters," Barbie reminded Skipper. "Especially when it's your best friend. And if she's truly your friend, she'll understand."

"You're right," replied Skipper. "I'm going to tell Courtney how we really feel about the outfits tomorrow. I just hope Drew and the others understand."

Chapter Four

The next day at school, Skipper was
nervous about what she would say to Courtney.
She wanted to be truthful, but she didn't want to
hurt her friend's feelings. She remembered that
Barbie sometimes wrote things down when she
was trying to solve a problem. At the top of a
piece of notebook paper, she wrote, *How to Tell
Courtney about the Outfits.* Skipper began her list:

1. The costumes are too flashy.
2. The guys feel silly wearing rhinestones.
3. Cara thinks they're too bright.

Skipper's thoughts were interrupted by the school bell. "Oh, well. Here goes nothing," she sighed, gathering up her books.

Courtney had a big smile on her face as she waited for Skipper by the lockers. "So did you try on your outfit yet?" she asked.

"Well, sort of," Skipper said slowly.

"What do you mean?" Courtney replied.

Skipper took a deep breath. "Courtney, there's something I need to tell you," she began.

Just then, Skipper saw Drew coming down the hall.

Suddenly Skipper was having second thoughts about telling Courtney the truth. She could feel herself losing all her courage.

Courtney waved her hand in front of her friend's face. "Earth to Skipper. Do you read me? Over," she joked.

"I'm sorry, Courtney," Skipper apologized. "I'd better go. I just realized I'm going to be late

for a meeting at Drew's house if I don't leave right now."

"But weren't you going to tell me something about your outfit?" Courtney asked.

"It's nothing," answered Skipper. She smiled at Courtney and tossed her books inside her locker.

"You're sure?" Courtney asked. "Because I can add more rhinestones if you want."

"No, don't do that," Skipper replied quickly. She slammed her locker shut. "I've really got to go, Courtney."

"Okay," Courtney agreed. She looked at her watch. "Yikes! I've gotta go, too! I'm going to be late for my design class."

Courtney raced down the hall away from her friend. "I'll talk to you tomorrow!" she called over her shoulder.

Chapter Five

Skipper ran up the steps to Drew's house and rang the doorbell. She heard laughter coming from inside.

"Come in!" Drew shouted.

Cara, Ron, and Drew were sitting in the living room, snacking on potato chips and soda.

"Hi, Skip," said Drew. "We were just taking turns coming up with different things we could do with these outfits." He held up the sparkling red one. "How about making a bike reflector out of this one?"

Drew picked up the green outfit and studied

30

it. "You know, I think I'll save this one for Halloween. I've always wanted to dress up as a **leprechaun,**" he joked.

Ron and Cara giggled.

"What can Skipper's outfit be?" Cara asked.

Skipper smiled halfheartedly. She didn't like making fun of her friend's hard work. She started to get angry and a little impatient. "Guys, we have a real problem here," she began.

"I know what you mean," said Drew. He held up the gold-studded shirt against his chest. "I can't wear this. I'll be arrested for **impersonating** a star in the Milky Way!"

"Come on," Skipper pleaded. "I'm serious."

"Okay, okay," Drew agreed. "But we've got to do something about these clothes. Any thoughts?"

"Maybe we could hire someone to steal them!" Ron joked.

Drew snapped his fingers. "That's it!" he

exclaimed. "Let's tell Courtney that the clothes were stolen from my dad's car last night."

"We can't tell her that!" Skipper cried.

"Why not?" asked Cara. "She'd feel awful if we told her we hated her outfits."

Skipper wasn't so sure. She didn't want to hurt Courtney's feelings. But lying to her best friend wasn't right, either. "What if Courtney finds out we lied?" she asked. "Then she'll *really* be hurt."

"She won't find out. All we have to do is keep our story straight," Drew replied. "Let's stick together on this. Can we count on you, Skipper?"

Skipper glanced around the room. Everyone was waiting for her answer.

Skipper's eyes rested on Drew's face. She didn't want to say no to him. Finally she nodded. "Okay," she said quietly.

"Good," Drew stated. "I knew you were one of us, Skip."

Then Drew turned to Ron. "I want to show you my new **amplifier** before we go to rehearsal. It will make our band as loud as Quick Sand!" he told his friend.

"Cool!" Ron replied, grabbing his crutches. "Let's go." Then the boys headed for the garage.

Chapter Six

Later that day after rehearsal, Skipper slowly walked home from Courtney's house. Her eyes ached from blinking back tears. She had barely been able to whisper good-bye to the others before leaving. When Skipper arrived home, she found a note from Barbie. She, Stacie, and Kelly were at the grocery store. The house was dark and quiet. Nellie, the family cat, rubbed up against Skipper's leg and purred loudly.

"I'm glad someone likes me," Skipper said, cradling Nellie in her arms. "Courtney wouldn't, if she knew what kind of friend I really am!"

Skipper went into her bedroom. She set Nellie down on the bed next to her.

"I need to talk to Barbie," Skipper sighed, petting Nellie's soft fur. "She'll know what to do."

Just then, Skipper heard the front door open. Her sisters were home.

Skipper was heading downstairs when the telephone rang. Barbie answered it.

"Hello? Oh, hi," Barbie said into the telephone. She waved when she saw Skipper. "Oh, that's great!" Barbie continued. Skipper saw her sister's face light up. "Please set up a meeting for nine A.M. See you then." Barbie hung up the phone. She had a big grin on her face.

"What was that all about?" Skipper asked.

"That was my assistant," Barbie answered. "She told me that one of my junior architects, who was going to quit, changed her mind. I had looked at several of her drawings today and asked her to make a lot of changes. She was upset."

35

Barbie explained to Skipper that she had given her suggestions in a very positive way. But her architect was sensitive. Barbie knew she had to be honest with her. She told her what was good about the drawings. But she also pointed out the things she didn't like.

Barbie shook her head. "If I'm not honest about their work, my architects won't learn and grow," she explained. "But I'm glad that Michelle has decided to stay. She's really good at drawing plans, but sometimes she overdoes things. I'll need to be extra-patient and give her plenty of **encouragement** and help."

Skipper rested her head on Barbie's shoulder. "I really need your help, too, Barbie."

Barbie put her arm around her sister. "I was just about to put away the groceries and then make myself a cup of hot cocoa. Want to join me?" she suggested.

Skipper smiled. "That sounds really nice."

"So what's going on?" Barbie asked, as the two sisters sat down with their steaming mugs.

Skipper frowned. "I feel just awful," she admitted. She told Barbie about the plan to lie to Courtney.

"I don't understand," said Barbie. "I thought you were going to tell Courtney the truth."

"I chickened out," Skipper confessed. "But I haven't told you the worst part. The band doesn't want Courtney to know the truth because they're afraid she'll kick us out of her dad's studio. Then we'd have nowhere to rehearse."

"Skipper," Barbie said seriously, "what do you think is the right thing to do?"

"I think the group should tell Courtney the truth," Skipper replied. "She might get a little upset. Okay, maybe she'll be very upset. But I know she'll understand. Maybe she could even fix the outfits if she knows what we don't like."

Barbie placed her hand on Skipper's

shoulder. "Then maybe you should explain that to Drew and the others," she said. "Courtney deserves to be told the truth, don't you think?"

Skipper nodded. "It's just like when you told that architect how you felt about her work." She thought for a moment. "I know you're right, Barbie. It's just that I really like being in the band." Skipper paused.

"And?" Barbie said, raising an eyebrow.

Skipper's face turned red, and she looked away.

Barbie touched her sister's chin and asked, "Are you blushing?"

The teenager's face turned even redder. "And I really like Drew," she blurted out. "I'm worried that the band might start looking for another drummer if I speak up."

"Wait a minute," Barbie stated. "If the people in the band are as cool as you say they are, then they will respect your **opinion.** If not, you might want to ask yourself if you really want to have them as friends."

Skipper nodded. "You're right. I'll do it," she declared. She gave her sister a hug and ran upstairs to her room.

"I'm proud of you, Skipper," Barbie called after her.

Skipper wiped her sweaty palms on her skirt. Then she picked up the phone and dialed Drew's number.

Drew answered the phone. "Hello?"

"Drew, it's Skipper," she began.

"Hi, Skip. What's up?" he replied.

"Drew, I've been doing a lot of thinking lately," she explained. "I don't want to lie to Courtney about the outfits being stolen." Skipper took a deep breath. Then she stated, "Courtney is my best friend. If the band doesn't want to tell her the truth, then I'll tell her myself."

There was silence on the other end of the line. Finally Drew spoke. "If that's how you really feel, I guess we can figure something out. Let's meet tomorrow after school in the studio. I'll phone the rest of the band. You call Courtney."

Skipper hung up the phone and smiled. She knew she had done the right thing. She suddenly felt much better!

Chapter Seven

The next day, Velvet Groove met at the studio after school. Ron's splint had been removed, and Cara's voice was back to normal. The practice flew by as the group worked on the hard parts of each of its songs. Then the friends waited for Courtney.

"Boy, I hope Courtney doesn't get too upset," said Cara.

Drew pretended to cry. "Good-bye, studio!" he joked, wiping his eyes with the corner of his shirt. "It was nice while it lasted!"

Skipper smiled and shook her head. "You're

not giving Courtney enough credit," she said. "She'll be okay with this. Really."

Just then, Courtney walked into the studio. "What's up, guys?" she asked, tossing her sketch pad on the table.

"It's about the outfits, Courtney," Skipper began. "They're not quite what we had in mind."

"I see," Courtney said slowly. "What don't you like about them?"

Skipper began by telling Courtney the good things about the costumes. They liked the velvet fabric. They also liked some of the colors.

Then Drew jumped in. "It's just that they're a little too fancy," he said.

"And sparkly," Ron added.

"And bright," Cara chimed in.

Courtney raised her hand. "Okay, I get it," she said, sounding angry.

"We're sorry, Courtney," Skipper apologized. "We should have told you from the beginning how we felt about them."

"I wish you had," Courtney told them. "I worked so hard on them!"

"We know you did, and we're really sorry," Cara said softly. Drew and Ron apologized, too.

Skipper touched her best friend's shoulder. "I can understand if you're angry with us," she told her.

Courtney shrugged. "Well, I'm glad you decided to tell me." Then she laughed and gave Skipper a playful nudge. "Come on! You're my best friend, Skip. And Velvet Groove is the best band. How could I let a bunch of rhinestones come between us?"

Skipper hugged Courtney. "I'm glad you feel that way," Skipper sighed with relief.

"You know," Courtney began, "I would have been happy to design the outfits any way you wanted me to."

"Courtney, I think they'll be fine with a

few changes," Skipper replied.

Cara, Ron, and Drew looked worried. "Don't look so scared, you guys," Skipper laughed. "Courtney, get your sketch pad. Come on, let's all work together!"

Everybody sat in a circle on the floor. Courtney listened carefully as the band members gave suggestions.

"I like the colors you chose," Skipper said. "But maybe we could have different shirts."

"Not so shiny," Cara offered.

Drew and Ron nodded their heads. "And without all those rhinestones," Drew added.

"The '60s look is really in," Courtney suggested. "What do you think of this?" she said as she began sketching her new ideas for the band.

Skipper watched eagerly as Courtney drew. She loved what she saw. And when she saw the smiles on the other band members' faces, she knew they did, too.

Finally Courtney finished.

"Well?" Courtney asked, holding up the sketches. "Do you like them? Be honest!"

"Yes!" Skipper and the others exclaimed together.

"Good!" Courtney said. "Now we've just got to make them in time for the dance!"

"I know who can help us out," Skipper stated with a smile.

Skipper raced upstairs to the phone. Minutes later, she returned. "Barbie offered to help us with the outfits," she announced. "She's going to pick us up and take us to Flower Power. It's a store that sells all kinds of stuff from the '60s. We should be able to find things there for Courtney's designs."

Soon Courtney and the band piled into Barbie's van and headed for Flower Power. Everyone had fun picking out daisy and peace sign **appliqués** and trying on flowered vests.

Barbie drove the group back to her house. They laid out the supplies and the old outfits on the living room floor. Cara, Ron, Courtney, and Barbie started taking the rhinestones off the shirts while Skipper and Drew made tacos for dinner. When the tacos were finished, Skipper and Drew brought them into the living room.

"Time to eat, everyone," Skipper announced, placing the food on the coffee table.

"All right!" said Ron. "This design work sure makes me hungry."

"When *aren't* you hungry?" Skipper joked with a twinkle in her eye. The group laughed as they gathered around the table to eat.

The next two weeks were very busy. There were rehearsals in Courtney's basement every afternoon, and sewing circles in Skipper's living room at night. Even Stacie and Kelly "helped" by modeling the new designs for the band.

Finally the big day arrived.

That morning at breakfast, Skipper said to Barbie, "I have butterflies in my stomach!"

"They'll go away once you're onstage. You'll see," Barbie told her.

"Promise?" Skipper asked.

"I promise," Barbie replied. "Velvet Groove is going to rock tonight!"

All day in school, Skipper had trouble concentrating. After school, Courtney's dad helped the band set up their **instruments** in the cafeteria.

That night, Skipper's heart pounded with excitement as she got ready for the dance. Barbie helped with her hair and makeup. Skipper asked her to make a long braid down her back, just like Lily Sands's. Then Skipper put on her outfit.

"You look great, Sis!" Barbie declared. "That top really makes your eyes sparkle!"

Skipper smiled. "Let's go!"

Barbie had volunteered to drive the band to the dance.

"You look better than Lily Sands!" Courtney announced, seeing Skipper.

Skipper hugged her best friend and said, "Thanks to you!"

Before long, Skipper and her friends were on their way to the school cafeteria.

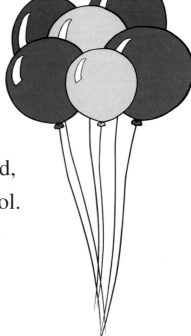

"Hey, the place looks fantastic!" Skipper exclaimed, standing in front of the school.

The building was lit by spotlights. Dozens of shiny silver and blue balloons decorated the doorway. Groups of friends hurried inside. Skipper could feel the excitement in the air.

The group thanked Barbie for the ride. Then

they ran toward the cafeteria.

"Hold on, Skipper!" Drew called.

Skipper stopped running. For a moment, the two were alone.

"Skipper, there's something I want to tell you," Drew said.

"What is it?" Skipper asked. She was sure he could hear her heart pounding.

Drew smiled shyly. "I just want you to know that it was really cool of you to stand up for Courtney. It would have been unfair to lie to her. You were right all along."

"Thanks," Skipper replied. "I'm glad you understood." Then she giggled. "I was afraid you guys were going to kick me out of the band!"

"And lose the best drummer in school? No way!" said Drew. "One other thing," he added. "I was wondering if you wanted to go to the movies next Friday. A bunch of us are planning to see *Attack of the Killer Turtles.*"

"I'd love to," Skipper replied, "but I've already made plans to spend Friday night with Courtney."

"No problem," Drew told her. "Would Courtney like to come along?"

Just then, Courtney walked up to them. "Did I hear my name?" she asked.

"Yes," Skipper replied. "Drew invited us to go see *Attack of the Killer Turtles* next Friday night."

"Sounds great!" Courtney exclaimed. Suddenly her face lit up. "Hey, I've got a terrific idea! Why don't we wear special outfits to the movie? We could all wear green football helmets and green down jackets, and dress up as killer turtles. We could even wear green eye shadow all over our faces!"

Skipper and Drew stared at Courtney in silence.

Courtney stopped. "Can't you guys take a

joke?" she exclaimed. "Come on, you didn't think I was serious, did you?"

Skipper and Drew looked at each other and started to laugh. Then the three friends hurried off to the cafeteria. The audience was waiting for Velvet Groove!